No More Hitting
for Little
Hamster!

Bernette Ford and Sam Williams

Boxer Books

Little Hamster heard bouncing.

He ran outside.

"Can I play, too?" he asked Ducky.

Ducky stopped bouncing her ball.

"No, you can't!" she said.
"Every time we play, you hit me."

Little Hamster's eyes filled with tears.

He hit Ducky, right on her arm.

He hit her as hard as he could.

"See!" said Ducky. "Don't hit!
Hitting hurts me!"

Ducky turned around
and marched into her house.
She took the ball, too.
Little Hamster felt cross.

Then Little Hamster
heard skipping.

It was Piggy.
Little Hamster
ran up to him.

"Let me play," said Little Hamster.

"You can't play with me," said Piggy.

"You always hit, and that hurts."

Little Hamster stamped his foot.

He was so cross that he punched Piggy,
right on his round little tummy.

Then Little Hamster ran away.

"No hitting!" Piggy cried after him.

"I told you! Hitting hurts."

Little Hamster ran until

he came to Lambkin's garden.

Lambkin was building a house.
"Let me play with you,"
said Little Hamster.

"Oh, no," said Lambkin.
"You might hit me —
you always hit!"

Little Hamster was very cross now.

He balled up his fist.

Then he hit Lambkin —

really hard —

right on her bottom.

"No one wants to play with you," she said. "You hit, and it hurts." Lambkin took her blocks inside. Little Hamster sat down and started to cry.

"What's wrong, Little Hamster?"
asked Bunny.

"Nobody will play with me," he cried.

"Everybody says I always hit.

It made me so cross that

I hit them all, really hard!"

"I will play with you," said Bunny.
"But you have to promise not to hit me."

"I promise," Little Hamster sniffled.
He kept his hands busy
playing with Bunny's skittles.
"See," he said. "I'm not hitting."
They had fun together.

Along came Ducky, Piggy,

and Lambkin.

"Don't play with him," said Ducky.

"He hits!" said Piggy.

Bunny said, "Little Hamster

is playing nicely.

He promised not to hit,
even if he gets cross."

"Can we play, too?"
asked Lambkin.

So they all played together.
And they had a wonderful time!
"No more hitting!"
promised Little Hamster.
"No hitting anyone, anymore!"

700003841240

For Fran
BF

For Sam and those special hamsters
SW

First published in Great Britain in 2011
by Boxer Books Limited.
www.boxerbooks.com

The illustrations were prepared using watercolor pans and charcoal on Aquarelle Arches hot press 180lb paper.
The text is set in Adobe Garamond.

ISBN 978-1-907152-99-3

1 3 5 7 9 10 8 6 4 2

Printed in China

All of our papers are sourced from managed forests and renewable resources.